Chip's Playground

The Hike
Ends Here!

Grassy
Meadow

Camp
Canyon

South Pond

Bird Tent

Donated by

FRIENDS OF THE
PALMER PUBLIC LIBRARY

Elliot's Park

Haunted Hike

BY PATRICK CARMAN
ILLUSTRATED BY JIM MADSEN

Palmer Public Library
655 S. Valley Way
Palmer, Alaska 99645

Orchard Books
An Imprint of Scholastic Inc. ❧ New York

For Reece Carman and Ken Geist,
two people who love Elliot's Park
as much as I do!

Text copyright © 2008 by Patrick Carman. • Illustrations copyright © 2008 by James Madsen. • All rights reserved. Published by Orchard Books, an imprint of Scholastic Inc., *Publishers since 1920.* ORCHARD BOOKS and design are registered trademarks of Watts Publishing Group, Ltd., used under license. SCHOLASTIC and associated logos are trademarks and/or registered trademarks of Scholastic Inc. No part of this publication may be reproduced, stored in a retrieval system, or transmitted in any form or by any means, electronic, mechanical, photocopying, recording, or otherwise, without written permission of the publisher.

For information regarding permission, write to Orchard Books, Scholastic Inc., Permissions Department, 557 Broadway, New York, NY 10012.

Library of Congress Cataloging-in-Publication Data

Carman, Patrick. Haunted hike / Patrick Carman. — 1st ed. p. cm. — (Elliot's park)
Summary: On Halloween night, while Ranger Canyon leads three small Squirrel Scouts on a haunted hike, Daisy sees a ghost and Elliot and his friends help investigate.
ISBN-13: 978-0-545-01931-6 (reinforced lib. bdg.) ISBN-10: 0-545-01931-1 (reinforced lib. bdg.) [1. Haunted places—Fiction. 2. Ghosts—Fiction. 3. Halloween—Fiction. 4. Squirrels—Fiction. 5. Scouting (Youth activity)—Fiction.] I. Title.
PZ7.C21694Hau 2008 [Fic]—dc22 2007030851

Printed in Mexico   49

10 9 8 7 6 5 4 3 2 1   08 09 10 11 12

Reinforced Binding for Library Use

First edition, August 2008

Art type ink and digital

Cover illustration copyright © by 2008 by James Madsen

Book design by Alison Klapthor

CHAPTERS

CHAPTER 1

The Rules!

It was Halloween in Elliot's Park, and three small Squirrel Scouts were sitting on a tree stump. They were waiting for Ranger Canyon to begin the haunted hike.

"I wonder when we get to leave," whispered Autumn. She was the smallest of the Squirrel

Scouts. Autumn was dressed as a cheerleader, with a big pom-pom in each hand.

"When it gets dark," said Lefty. He was wearing a little black robe, tied with a belt. He was a ninja.

"I don't like the dark!" said Daisy. She had white wings, a daisy chain necklace, and fairy dust in her tail.

"HELLO, SCOUTS!" cried Ranger Canyon. Autumn yelped and tossed her big pom-poms into the air. They got stuck in a tree.

Daisy fell off the stump and fairy dust flew everywhere. Lefty sneezed not once but three times. The fairy dust had tickled his nose.

"It's only me," said Ranger Canyon. He scampered up the tree trunk and found Autumn's pom-poms. "No need to be afraid."

All the scouts settled back into their spots on the tree stump.

"Can any of you tell me the reason for the haunted hike?" asked Ranger Canyon.

"We earn scout badges!" yelled Lefty.

All the scouts nodded. They loved earning scout badges more than just about anything.

"And how do we earn scout badges?"

Autumn raised her paw and shook one of her pom-poms really fast. It made a shaky sound.

"I know!" she said.

Ranger Canyon called on Autumn.

"Having the best costume!" Autumn said.

"Or telling a scary story at the campfire," piped in Lefty. He jumped up and karate-chopped the tree stump. "Like 'The Haunted Ninja'!"

Lefty rubbed his little paw. The tree stump was harder than he'd expected.

"And how else can you earn scout badges?" asked Ranger Canyon. He was looking at Daisy.

"Will the haunted hike be scary?" she asked. Daisy was shaking a little bit because she was afraid.

Before Ranger Canyon could answer, Autumn yelled out the last way to earn a scout badge.

"Finishing the haunted hike!"

"That's right," said Ranger Canyon. "I think you're all going to earn at least one new badge tonight. Let's get going!"

And so the haunted hike began. Ranger Canyon led the way. Autumn cheered them on. Lefty *chop-chop-chopped* at the falling leaves. And Daisy tried her best to be brave.

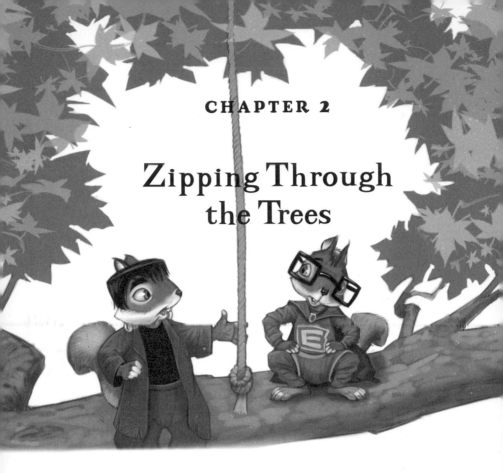

CHAPTER 2

Zipping Through
the Trees

Halloween is a special time in Elliot's
Park. All the squirrels get dressed up. Lots and
lots of leaves are falling. And best of all,
everyone rides the rope swing!

"I'll let you go first this year," said Chip.

He was dressed as Frankensquirrel, his favorite monster.

"I'm not going first. You go first!" said Elliot. He was not as brave as his best friend, Chip.

It was a really long rope. And it was very high off the ground.

"Mister Nibbles did just fine," said Chip. "You have nothing to worry about."

They had already put a little cape on Mister Nibbles and sent him zooming through the trees. But as everyone in Elliot's Park knew by now, Mister Nibbles was a stuffed animal.

Chip eyed Elliot from his head to his feet. "You look like you can fly."

Elliot was wearing red underwear over bright blue tights. He had a matching blue cape. He was Super Squirrel.

"I can fly. I just want you to go first."

Chip loved riding on the rope. He was

secretly glad Elliot was afraid to go first.

"If you say so!"

Chip held the rope between his paws.

He took a deeeeeeep breath. He winked at Elliot.

"Here goes!" he shouted.

But just as Chip was about to soar off the tree, he saw Crash flying toward them. Crash was the only flying squirrel in the park. She had problems landing.

"Watch out!" cried Elliot.

Crash was wearing a Dracula cape and a spiffy red bow tie. She was out of control as usual.

"She's coming in too fast!" cried Elliot. "Duck!"

Elliot and Chip closed their eyes and ducked.

Crash grabbed the rope above their heads. She spun around in a circle. And then—*boing!*—shot straight up into the air.

"Where'd she go?" Chip opened his eyes.

But there was no time to answer. Crash landed right on top of him.

"Sorry, old chap," said Crash. She brushed herself off and straightened her bow tie. "Someone's put up a booby trap."

"That's not a booby trap. It's a rope swing!" cried Chip.

Crash gazed at the long line running up into the trees. She didn't understand.

"It's for flying," said Chip.

"Oh!" said Crash, ruffling her wing-like arms. "What a clever idea!"

Looking down, Elliot spotted a band of three merry Squirrel Scouts crossing the park. They were led by Ranger Canyon, the park's scout leader. All of them were dressed up for Halloween.

"Where are you off to?" yelled Elliot from way up in the tree.

"Camp Canyon!" cried Autumn.

"Why are you way up there in the tree?" yelled Lefty.

"Because we're going to fly!" said Chip.

"You can't fly! You're a squirrel," said Daisy.

"Only Crash can fly," Autumn replied.

"She's a flying squirrel."

The Squirrel Scouts loved Crash. They thought she was the niftiest thing in the park.

Seeing the Squirrel Scouts had given Chip an idea.

"I think Elliot can fly even faster than Crash!" he yelled.

All the Squirrel Scouts laughed. Daisy's tail twitched again, sending more fairy dust into the air. Lefty sneezed.

"How about a race between Crash and Elliot?" asked Chip. He pointed his tiny paw. "Over to that tree."

"I'd be delighted!" said Crash. She scampered up the tree quick as could be and looked down. "Ready when you are!"

Elliot gulped. He pulled up on his red underpants.

"It's not as scary as it looks," said Chip.

Elliot glanced out over the open space between the trees.

It was a long way down.

"I'm not sure," said Elliot.

"You can do it!" yelled all the Squirrel Scouts from below.

But Elliot was too afraid. He held on to the rope, but he wouldn't jump. So Chip, being the best friend that he was, pushed Elliot off the tree.

And just like that, *zoooooom!* Elliot was flying through the air on the long rope.

"Tallyho!" cried Crash. She jumped into the air, chasing after Elliot. She caught a nice breeze and shot high into the air.

Then the breeze died and Crash dropped down toward the swishing rope.

She crashed into Elliot and held on tight.

They spun around and around in circles.

Elliot's cape wrapped around the rope. Crash's cape covered Elliot's eyes! And the rope swing kept going!

"How do you stop?" yelled Crash.

"You hit the tree on the other side!" said Elliot.

And that's just what they did. When the rope swing swooshed back the other way, Elliot and Crash came along. They were all tangled up in the rope.

When they finally came to a stop at the bottom they heard the sound of laughter.

"It's a tie!" yelled the young Squirrel Scouts. They kept laughing as they walked away.

But very soon the little Squirrel Scouts wouldn't be laughing anymore.

It was a long journey to Camp Canyon. The sky was getting darker.

And a Halloween ghost was about to visit Elliot's Park!

CHAPTER 3

Into the Field House

Ranger Canyon led the Squirrel Scouts through Elliot's Park. They zipped up the sides of trees. They zoomed down little paths. And then they arrived at the steps of an old house.

"It's the Field House!" said Lefty.

"Spooooooky!" said Daisy.

"What's it for?" asked Autumn.

"It's where people go to learn about leaves and trees and nuts," said Ranger Canyon, twirling his handlebar mustache. He hopped up the steps leading to the Field House door.

"In we go!" Ranger Canyon called. He opened a tiny door and disappeared inside.

The three Squirrel Scouts stood at the bottom of the steps. After a long silence, Daisy whispered, "This place is scary."

A light wind blew, making shadows dance everywhere.

"But we have to go inside," said Lefty, trying to be brave. "No Field House, no scout badge."

All three scouts looked at their little blue sashes.

"The scout badge is worth it," said Autumn. "Come on!"

Autumn darted up the stairs and vanished into the Field House. Lefty followed. Just then the sound of a night owl filled the air.

Whooooo, whooooo!

Daisy scampered up the old steps and through the tiny door.

"Now that we're all inside," said Ranger Canyon, "I'll close the door. We don't want any mice getting in."

The door slammed shut. Ranger Canyon began walking. "Off we go then—to the other side."

Ranger Canyon took the lead. It was a long way across the Field House and there were many things to see. Light crept in from the lamps in the park.

"Do you want to hear my Haunted Ninja story?" Lefty asked Autumn.

Autumn rolled her eyes. Lefty was always talking about ninjas.

"No. Do you want to hear my story? It's about a pinecone that comes to life in the park!"

"That sounds boring," said Lefty. He looked at Daisy. "What's your story about?"

Daisy didn't like haunted stories. But she liked adventure.

"It's about two big dogs that chase a little squirrel. But then the squirrel eats a magic walnut and it makes him bigger."

"How much bigger?" asked Autumn.

"As tall as the tallest tree in Elliot's Park."

"Wow!" said Lefty. "What happens then?"

"Well," said Daisy. "The dogs run away. They run right into the yellow house."

"The house where Mister Nibbles used to live?" asked Autumn.

"The very one!" answered Daisy.

"Double wow!" said Lefty. "Then what happens?"

"The giant squirrel picks up the house and shakes it until the dogs fall out."

Daisy looked up from telling her story. She'd walked almost all the way across the Field House.

"And then the dogs run away with their tails between their legs. They run all the way to Walla Walla!"

"Where's Walla Walla?" asked Autumn.

"Far, far away from Elliot's Park," said Daisy.

Lefty and Autumn thought Daisy's story was the best. It would be hard to beat at the campfire.

"What's that?!" cried Daisy suddenly. She grabbed her own tail and fairy dust filled the air. Lefty sneezed again.

"That's the BIG acorn," said Ranger Canyon. "The biggest to ever fall from a tree in Elliot's Park."

The BIG acorn was in a glass case.

There was a small light shining down on it.

"Come over here!" said Autumn. Her voice was far away. "Look at this!"

Lefty and Ranger Canyon followed Autumn's voice, but Daisy couldn't stop staring at the acorn. She liked acorns and wondered if she could get it open.

Light was pouring into the Field House. There were shadows moving on the walls. And then, suddenly, there was something else. It was outside, drifting across the window behind the BIG acorn.

"Hellllllp!!" yelled Daisy. She ran around in circles, her little wings flapping. Fairy dust flew everywhere.

"Hellllllp!!"

Lefty was the first to arrive. Ranger Canyon and Autumn were close behind.

"What's wrong?" asked Lefty.

Before Daisy could answer Lefty was
*HU . . . HU . . . HUCHEW*ing again.

Daisy ran out the door of the Field House.
She jumped down the steps.

"Ghost! I saw a ghost!!"

Squirrels came running from every
direction. All of them were dressed for trick-
or-treating.

"The Field House is haunted!" cried Daisy.

Elliot and his sister, Twitch, arrived on
the scene.

Crash flew in behind them.

Chip zoomed down the side of a tree.

"Haunted? Really haunted?" said Twitch,
hopping up and down. She was dressed in
a pink princess dress. In one hand she held a
soda pop. In the other was a glittery
magic wand.

"Yes, haunted!" said Daisy.

Lefty chopped the air with his paws like a ninja, just in case the ghost came back.

Pistachio had also arrived on the scene. He was wearing an eye patch and a pirate hat. He had a bag of nuts thrown over his shoulder.

"We better go inside and take a look around."

"Oh no!" said Chip. "You're not allowed in there."

Everyone knew that Pistachio LOVED all kinds of nuts. He wanted to get his paws on the BIG acorn.

Elliot spoke softly to Daisy.

"Why do you think the Field House is haunted?" he asked.

"I saw a ghost! It flew past the window. I saw it!" cried Daisy.

"There are a lot of shadows in there," said

Lefty. "Maybe you imagined it."

Daisy looked at all the faces around her. Everyone from Elliot's Park had arrived. They were all staring at her. And none of them believed her. She started to think maybe Lefty was right. But it had looked so real!

"I did see it!" said Daisy.

Elliot tried to make her feel better.

"It's a long way to Camp Canyon," he said. "Why don't you keep going? Chip and I will keep a lookout for ghosts. So will Crash."

Crash and Chip both nodded.

"We'll all keep a lookout!" said Twitch. Then she burped. It was a strawberry-flavored burp, just like the soda pop.

All of this watching for the ghost seemed to make Daisy feel a little better. When Ranger Canyon and the Squirrel Scouts were on their way again, Elliot turned to his friends.

"I'll meet you at the pond," he said. "Chip, you take the long way around. Crash, you fly overhead. And keep your eyes peeled!"

"Brilliant!" said Crash.

Elliot ran toward the pond in his Super
Squirrel costume. But he didn't feel super.

What if there really was a ghost in
Elliot's Park?

This could be the scariest Halloween ever!

CHAPTER 4

Rollie Hill

"**Let's go** that way!" said Lefty.

It was really dark now, but Lefty could see the outline of a rising hill of grass.

"I'll wait for you on the other side," said Ranger Canyon. He wanted the Squirrel Scouts to go over the hill by themselves.

"But I don't want to go alone!" cried Daisy. "Can't you go with us?"

It wasn't a very big hill. Ranger Canyon would be able to see Daisy walk up and over. He wanted her to be brave.

"I'll be close by," he said. "You can do it!"

Daisy wasn't so sure. But Lefty and Autumn encouraged her. And when she looked back to find Ranger Canyon, he was already gone.

"Here we go!" said Lefty.

The Squirrel Scouts made their way to the top of Rollie Hill. Rollie Hill was shaped like a jelly bean. Round on top, with a little curve in the middle. It was covered in soft green grass. And it was perfect for lying down and rolling!

"Let's roll!" said Lefty.

Lefty loved rolling down Rollie Hill

almost as much as he loved peanut butter.

"There's no time to play on Rollie Hill,"
said Daisy. She wanted to find Ranger
Canyon before another ghost appeared.

But Lefty was already halfway down
the hill. His tail made a *swoosh* and
then a *thump* as he rolled.
Swoosh thump swoosh
thump swoosh
thump!

When Lefty reached the bottom he tried to stand up and fell over. He sure was dizzy.

"Woooo-hoooo!" he laughed. Daisy and Autumn looked down from the top of the hill.

"That looks like fun," said Autumn. And then she was gone! Rolling down Rollie Hill with her pom-poms flying.

Daisy stood on top of the jelly bean–shaped hill all alone. She could see most of Elliot's Park from there. She looked back. And there it was! The ghost of Elliot's Park, flying through the trees!

"*AaAaAaAaaAaaaaa!*" Daisy shouted. She ran down Rollie Hill toward her friends. "Ghoooooooooost!" she cried.

When Daisy reached the bottom she jumped into Ranger Canyon's arms.

"I saw the ghost again!"

But no one seemed to believe her.

"Are you sure it was a ghost?" asked Ranger Canyon.

"Positive!" answered Daisy.

"Let's go back up there and have a look," said Lefty. "We can roll back down again!"

"I'm not going back up there!" said Daisy. She clung tighter to Ranger Canyon.

"Let's keep going," he said. "We're almost to the pond. And after that, we'll be at Camp Canyon. Maybe we'll see Elliot along the way. He'll know what to do about that pesky ghost."

This made Daisy feel a little better. Ranger Canyon set her down.

"Can you carry me next?" asked Lefty.

"Ninjas are never, ever carried," said Ranger Canyon. Lefty nodded, sure that their scout leader was right.

And so the scouts were on their way again. They went down the cobblestone path.

They went past the Fishin' Hole. They quietly
tiptoed by the bronze General's Cannon.

It wouldn't be long before they arrived at
the big pond in Elliot's Park.

CHAPTER 5

The Haunted Pond

"**Maybe** Scratchy Spurs can help me figure this out," Elliot said to himself.

He had zipped down the twisting path. He had climbed a tall tree. He had jumped from branch to branch. And finally, he had arrived at the pond.

Scratchy Spurs slept in an old tree by the water's edge, but he wasn't there.

"Where could Scratchy Spurs be?" said Elliot.

Honk! Honk! Hoooooonk!

It was Wilma, the biggest goose in the pond. She didn't like squirrels.

When Elliot glanced at Wilma he saw that she was wearing a silver ribbon around her neck.

"It's not easy getting a ribbon on a giant chicken."

The voice had come from a little bench down by the water.

"Scratchy Spurs!" cried Elliot.

Elliot's old friend was sitting on the bench. He was wearing the same things he always wore: spurs and a cowboy hat. But he had added a black mask around his tiny squirrel eyes. He was the Lone Ranger!

"Wilma drifts close to the shore when she sleeps," said Scratchy Spurs. He scratched the top of his foot with his twig cane.

"I had to be mighty quiet to fool a chicken that big. But Wilma needed a Halloween costume."

"You put that ribbon on Wilma?" asked Elliot.

"Sure did!" said Scratchy Spurs.

Elliot sat down next to his old friend.

"Have you seen anything strange tonight?" asked Elliot.

"Only an old goose wearing a silver ribbon!" said Scratchy Spurs. He scratched his ear. "Strange indeed."

"You haven't seen anything flying?" asked Elliot.

"Like what?" asked Scratchy Spurs.

"Like maybe a ghost?" asked Elliot.

He pulled up his red underpants again. They kept slipping down.

"That's a silly outfit you have there," said Scratchy Spurs.

"So is that mask," said Elliot. The two laughed at each other.

There was a noise from down the path.

"What's that?" said Elliot. He thought it might be the ghost. But it was only

Ranger Canyon and the Squirrel Scouts.
Ranger Canyon was carrying Lefty, who had
fallen asleep.

"Snack break!" cried the scout leader.
Wilma saw all the squirrels and blew her
horn again. *Honk! Honk!*

Lefty woke up and jumped right out of Ranger
Canyon's arms. He *chop-chop-chopped* the air.

"Who wants peanut butter?" asked Ranger
Canyon. All the scouts raised their paws.
Squirrels love peanut butter.

"Hello, Mister Spurs," said Autumn.
She had moved closer to him while Lefty
and Daisy smacked their little lips with
peanut butter.

"Hello, Autumn," said Scratchy Spurs.
"I see you're a cheerleader for Halloween."

"Yes, sir."

"Have you got any chicken cheers?"

Elliot rolled his eyes. Wilma was not a giant chicken. She was a goose. But Scratchy Spurs loved to tease mean old Wilma whenever he could.

"Oh yes, sir! I have a very good cheer for that."

Autumn raised her big pom-poms high in the air.

"Hey, all you chicken fans!
Stand up and clap your hands!"

All the squirrels clapped and laughed. Wilma honked louder than ever. Everyone looked out over the water.

And that's when it happened! They all saw it at once!

"It'th a ghotht!" cried Lefty. His mouth was so full of peanut butter he could hardly talk.

"A ghost!" said Elliot, pointing out over the pond. Even Wilma looked up as it flew over her head. It was not much bigger than Elliot. And it was white.

"I told you! I told you!" shouted Daisy, jumping up and down. Fairy dust flew off her tail.

Lefty had never sneezed with peanut butter in his mouth.

It was yucky. Everyone said, *"Eeeeewwwww!"* at the same time.

The ghost flew all the way across the pond. Then it vanished into the trees on the other side.

"Daisy was right!" cried Autumn. "Elliot's Park is haunted!"

But Scratchy Spurs wasn't so sure. He scratched his tummy. He scratched his elbow. Then he whispered something into Elliot's ear.

"I think you may be right!" said Elliot.

And then Elliot had an idea.

"We can teach this ghost a lesson if we all work together."

They all huddled together at the edge of the pond. Soon a plan was formed.

"We'd better get moving," said Elliot. "There's no time to waste."

Scratchy Spurs stood up and yelled out over the water.

"Hi-yo, Silver. Away!"

Wilma tried and tried to get the silver ribbon off. But it was really tied on too well.

Scratchy Spurs started down the path and Elliot cheered his old friend on.

"The Lone Ranger rides again!" he shouted while Scratchy climbed up on Wilma's back.

CHAPTER 6

Camp Canyon

The scouts didn't have to walk very
far before they came to Camp Canyon.
It was hidden in the trees next to the pond.
There were tiny tents around a tinier fire. There
were twigs for roasting mini marshmallows.
There were small stumps to sit on.

"That's mine!" yelled Lefty. He dove through the door of a red tent. He took off his backpack. Then he started dancing.

Daisy and Autumn shared a yellow tent. They rolled out their sleeping bags. It was like home away from home.

When the Squirrel Scouts came out of their tents, Elliot had arrived. Scratchy Spurs was with him.

"Gather around the fire," said Ranger Canyon. "Time for the scary story contest!"

Scratchy Spurs had a lot of great stories. He sat down by the fire. He scratched his nose. He took a deep breath.

"Many years ago," he began, "I rode a haunted horse in a haunted rodeo!"

All the Squirrel Scouts gasped.

"The haunted horse had never been ridden. But I aimed to ride it!"

Lefty, Autumn, and Daisy huddled closer together. Just then, something moved in the trees above.

"A ghost!" cried Elliot, pointing into the sky. And sure enough, there was a ghost!

Lefty ran for his tent and dove inside. Autumn and Daisy followed and dove in behind him.

"Oooooh noooo! It's the ghost of Elliot's Park!" yelled Daisy. Then she giggled nervously.

The Squirrel Scouts knew better by now. Elliot had already told them to look more carefully. Lefty pointed and all three peeked out of the tent. There, above the little tents, the ghost flew past. But it was not a ghost after all!

"See there," whispered Lefty. "It's on a rope. It's not real."

The three squirrels chuckled softly. Elliot ran around the fire, yelling.

"Help me! Help me! The ghost is back! *AaaAaAaAaa!*"

And then everyone heard a giggle from behind the trees. The ghost was gone, but the giggler was there!

"Come out from behind those trees!" cried Scratchy Spurs.

And there he was—Chip! He pulled the little white sheet off. Underneath he was still dressed in his Frankensquirrel costume. He was laughing so hard he fell over.

"So it was you all along," said Elliot.

Chip had let go of the long rope. It swung back and forth over Camp Canyon.

And then something happened that surprised even Chip. Another, even more real-looking ghost flew through the trees overhead!

"G-g-g-g-ghost!" said Chip. He wasn't laughing anymore.

"Very funny!" said Ranger Canyon. "You can't fool us that easily."

The ghost flew by again, only lower this time. It looked so real! Chip ran past the fire pit and dove into one of the tents.

"The park really is haunted! Hide, everyone! Hide!"

The ghost made one final pass. This time it flew a little too low. It crashed into a tent. The same tent Chip had jumped into!

The tent stakes came out of the ground.
The ropes tangled. Chip and the ghost were
rolling all over Camp Canyon!

"Helllllp!" cried Chip. Finally, after a long
time, Chip got free of the ghost and the tent.
He was about to run for the woods when the
ghost spoke.

"Sorry, old chap," said the ghost. "A bit
low on that last pass."

Chip turned back and saw Ranger Canyon
scowling at him.

Crash removed the white sheet from her
head and cried, "Tallyho!"

"I guess Elliot's Park isn't haunted after all," said Elliot.

Just then everyone came out from behind the trees. All the squirrels from Elliot's Park were staring at Chip. They all knew about the trick he had played on the Squirrel Scouts. Stitches, the park doctor, walked right up to Chip in her big red clown shoes. She was wearing a squishy red clown nose that made her sound funny.

"Don't scare little squirrels," she said. "That's not nice."

Chip nodded and smiled. "I've learned my lesson!"

He asked Autumn if he could borrow her pom-poms. When she'd handed them over, Chip held them high over his head. He looked very silly in his Frankensquirrel costume.

"Three cheers for the fearless Squirrel Scouts!" said Chip.

Everyone shouted, "Hip-hip-hurray! Hip-hip-hurray! Hip-hip-hurray!"

"And especially for Daisy— the bravest squirrel in Elliot's Park!" added Ranger Canyon.

Elliot and Chip raised Daisy on their shoulders.

"Hip-hip-hurray! Hip-hip-hurray! Hip-hip-hurray!"

And then the Halloween party started!

CHAPTER 7

The Haunted Hike
Scout Badges

The great big Elliot's Park Halloween party was in full swing.

Twitch and Pistachio were bobbing for acorns. Lefty swung back and forth on the rope overhead. Elliot watched and wished he wasn't so afraid to ride it.

Stitches and Autumn were running back and forth between the games. Autumn won pin-the-tail-on-the-poodle. Stitches won the pinecone toss.

And there was more!

Sparkle wore a tall black hat with moons and stars. She wore a long black robe to match.

"A full moon!" she shouted.

Stitches came over in her big red clown shoes and said, "I wonder if it's made of cheddar cheese?"

Sparkle wrinkled her nose. She was a stargazer. She knew better.

"It's made of Swiss cheese."

Everyone told their scary stories around the fire as they roasted mini marshmallows. Chip held Mister Nibbles tightly, in case Mister Nibbles got scared. And Daisy's BIG squirrel story won first place. A silver scout badge was pinned to her blue sash.

"Your attention, please!" shouted Ranger Canyon. "Chip has something he'd like to say."

Chip called Daisy, Lefty, and Autumn to stand with him.

"For teaching me an important lesson," he began. "And for completing the haunted hike," he continued, "three super-shiny scout badges!"

Ranger Canyon pinned a bright golden badge on each sash. Everyone cheered.

"And for Elliot," said Ranger Canyon. Elliot came forward and stood next to the Squirrel Scouts. "For solving our ghost mystery . . . a merit badge for you, too!"

Ranger Canyon pinned the badge on Elliot's cape.

"No more ghosts in Elliot's Park!" cried Chip. More cheers!

"And finally," said Ranger Canyon. "The best costume prize is a tie! The scout badges go to Autumn, Lefty, Daisy, and . . . Frankensquirrel!"

Chip could hardly believe it. He ran right up and stood in line with the Squirrel Scouts. Every squirrel loves a shiny new trinket!

When it was quiet again, there was a rustling in the dark. From deep in the woods . . . a floating cowboy hat!

"It's the haunted horse!" cried Chip. He clutched Mister Nibbles and dove into one of the tents.

Scratchy Spurs came out from behind a tree, twirling his cowboy hat on the end of his twig cane.

"Who was that masked squirrel?" asked Elliot.

Everyone laughed. Elliot thought about how much he loved his park. He looked at the scout badge pinned to his cape. He pulled up his red underwear. Then he darted up into the trees to ride the swinging rope.

"*Wooooooo-hooooooooo!*" he cried as he zoomed through the trees.

His fear of riding the long rope had vanished. Just like the ghost of Elliot's Park!

CAST OF

Chip (Frankensquirrel)

Chip is a bit bigger than other squirrels and

he loves all kinds of sports. He has a history of major accidents, including the time he chipped one of his two large front teeth on the monkey bar. Chip is a daredevil and will try anything. *Distinguishing features: two large front teeth, one chipped; Elliot's best friend.*

Crash (Dracula)

Crash is the only flying squirrel in Elliot's

Park. She has trouble with her landing skills. She says she is only stopping by on a planned flight around the world. But she always has a good reason for staying. Crash loves to tell about all the places she's been. *Distinguishing features: the only flying squirrel of the bunch; British accent, flying goggles, and often has trouble landing.*

Daisy (fairy), Lefty (ninja), and Autumn (cheerleader)

All three are young, resourceful, and highly competitive scouts. They are always performing tasks to earn Canyon Squirrel Scout merit badges. *Distinguishing features: bright blue merit badge sashes.*

Elliot (Super Squirrel)

Elliot is a very smart squirrel who lives inside

the largest tree in the park. Whenever a problem arises, Elliot solves it, with the help of his friends. A lovable nerd. *Distinguishing features: big black glasses; he usually wears a collared shirt with a wide tie.*

Mister Nibbles

Mister Nibbles is not an ordinary squirrel; he's

a stuffed animal squirrel. When you press his ear he says five different things. All the other squirrels in the park think Mister Nibbles is hilarious. *Distinguishing features: stuffed; he does not move and says only five things.*

Pistachio (pirate)

Pistachio is a nut lover. He will forcibly take nuts from anyone who enters the park eating them. He is often seen being chased up a tree by parents and dogs. *Distinguishing features: always eating, hiding, or trying to open a nut of one kind or another.*

Ranger Canyon

Canyon is the Park Ranger squirrel, also a Squirrel Scout leader. He gives out merit badges to Squirrel Scouts for completing park assignments. *Distinguishing features: a Park Ranger tie and a handlebar mustache.*

Scratchy Spurs (the Lone Ranger)

Scratchy Spurs is a retired rodeo squirrel who

dreams of riding one last time. He is the oldest and wisest squirrel in Elliot's Park. Scratchy Spurs and Elliot are buddies. *Distinguishing features: spurs, battered cowboy hat, grass in mouth, twig cane; he speaks with a southern accent.*

Stitches (clown)

Stitches is the park doctor. She is especially

well liked by everyone. *Distinguishing features: white coat and stethoscope around her neck.*

Sparkle (witch)

Sparkle loves stargazing. She likes to be out at night. *Distinguishing feature: star-shaped earrings.*

Twitch (princess)

Twitch is Elliot's sister. She loves any type of  sugar, especially soda pop of any flavor. She is very good at finding soda pop. She is hyper almost all of the time. *Distinguishing features: jangling soda pop–top necklace; runs around a lot and is very good at burping.*

Wilma

Wilma is the biggest goose on the pond in  Elliot's Park. She does not like anyone, especially squirrels. *Distinguishing features: big, white, and loves to honk.*

ELLIOT'S PARK
Ghost Decorations

SUPPLIES:

- Paper dinner napkins
- Tissues
- String, thread, or yarn
- Black magic marker

DIRECTIONS:

1. Open up a dinner napkin.

2. Put two to three balled-up tissues in the middle of the unfolded napkin.

3. Tie a string around the napkin with the tissues inside.

4. Decorate the head of the ghost with the black magic marker.

5. Hang up your ghost and watch it fly.

How to Make the Shadow of Chip Frankensquirrel

SUPPLIES:

- White paper
- Black construction paper
- Safety scissors
- Flashlight
- Scotch tape

STEP 1

On the white paper, trace the outline of Chip Frankensquirrel from page 69.

STEP 2

Place the white paper over the black construction paper and cut Chip Frankensquirrel out of both sheets.

STEP 3

Be careful you don't cut off the bolts on his neck!

STEP 4

Tape the black Chip Frankensquirrel to the flashlight lens with clear tape.

STEP 5

Turn on the flashlight and project the image of your Frankensquirrel on the wall.

RANGER CANYON'S SCAVENGER HUNT

SUPPLIES:

- Clear plastic bags with ties or zips
- Marker, pencil, or pen
- A pad for notes and/or drawing
- Big bag to hold found items

A fun activity to do in a local park is to get your schoolteacher to take your class on a Ranger Canyon Scavenger Hunt. Divide your class into teams. Try to find some ways that your park is like Elliot's Park. Collect acorns, pinecones, leaves, rocks, and other fun objects. Make notes or draw pictures of all the different kinds of nature you discover (like frogs at the edge of a pond or old birds' nests), and show off what you have collected from the park when you get back to class. See what team has won Ranger Canyon's Scavenger Hunt!

**Get ready for the
World Squirrel Soccer Championship
in the next Elliot's Park,
*The Walnut Cup!***

From *The Walnut Cup*

The Teams Arrive!

Flowers were beginning to bloom. Birds were singing. The grass had turned bright green. It was spring in Elliot's Park! And that meant something BIG was about to happen.

"Bravo! Here comes the team from Brazil!" shouted Crash.

Elliot looked up in the air and saw Crash

flying overhead. Crash was the only flying squirrel in the park.

"Where?" cried Elliot. "I don't see them."

"And the German team! And the Italian team! And the Swedish team! And the . . ."

Crash wasn't watching where she was going. She flew right into the branches of a big tree. It made a lot of noise.

"Are you all right?" cried Elliot from below. The branches moved back and forth above him. They were filled with tiny new leaves. Crash's head poked out into the open.

"Jolly good!"

Elliot's best friend, Chip, was coming toward them. He was dribbling a walnut between his feet. Chip kicked it *really* hard and *really* high and it went sailing into the tree. Crash dodged the walnut but lost her balance and fell backward. When Elliot looked up, Crash was hanging by one paw.

"I see our captain has arrived," Crash said. Her goggles were crooked on her nose.

Chip smiled and retrieved the walnut. They were all dressed in bright blue Elliot's Park soccer jerseys.

"Let's go welcome the teams to the park," said Elliot.

"This year we're going to win it all!" said Chip. Chip liked to win things. He was the captain of the team. But Elliot wasn't so sure. A lot of great teams came to the Walnut Cup.

"Do you really think we can win?" asked Elliot. Chip juggled the walnut between his little knees as they walked.

"Are you kidding? We're the best team ever!"

Chip let the walnut hit the ground. He kicked it *really* hard and *really* high. It sailed out into the open and landed on the far end of the soccer field. One of the Brazilians flicked it into the air. He bounced it off his head, his heel, his knee, and then to one of his teammates. The walnut went around and around between them. All the Brazilians laughed.

"Tricky footwork," said Elliot.

"Nothing we can't handle," said Chip.

As they came closer, Crash flew low and tumbled over and over again across the field. She did about ten flips and came to a stop. The rest of the Elliot's Park team, Sparkle, Stitches, and Elliot's sister Twitch, was already on the field practicing.

Twitch was bouncing up and down. Her lips were orange.

"You've been drinking soda pop, haven't you?" asked Elliot.

Twitch nodded. Then she burped. It was

an orange-flavored burp. She was very happy.

Elliot turned his attention to the visiting teams. Brazil, Germany, Sweden, and Italy were already kicking walnuts all over the field. France, Japan, and Spain were just arriving. Including Elliot's team, that made eight teams. And there were six squirrels on every team. That was a lot of squirrels!

"Welcome to Elliot's Park!" said Elliot. "The tournament begins in one hour!"

Everyone cheered. Squirrels love soccer.

"And de game ball? Where is de game ball?" asked one of the Brazilians. The home team had to provide a *perfectly* round walnut. It was a rule. If Elliot didn't have one, his team wouldn't be allowed to play. They'd lose before they even started!

Chip still had the same walnut he'd been kicking all over the park. One of the German players stepped forward. He was looking at the walnut.

"Das is de game ball?" she asked.

The two strikers for the Swedish team also inspected the walnut. Their names were Sven and Olga.

"Shape like egg," said Sven. "Must be *round.*"

The Italians also piped in.

"Where is round ball? And spaghetti. Where is the spaghetti?"

The Italians love pasta.

"Not to worry!" said Elliot. "I have a *very* round walnut for the tournament. I've been saving it all winter just for today. It's *perfect!*"

Elliot thought about the sound he'd heard all winter long. *Crack! Crack! Crack!* It was the sound of walnuts being opened. Almost all the walnuts had already been eaten. Even egg-shaped practice walnuts were hard to find. Saving a perfectly round walnut all winter long was a big deal. Everyone began to practice while Elliot ran home to get the *perfectly* round walnut. It was hidden in his tree house.

Little did Elliot know that someone was secretly following him. It was someone who LOVED walnuts even more than soccer. Someone who'd been listening and watching from high up in a tree. It was a squirrel named Pistachio!

About the Author
Patrick Carman

Patrick Carman created the world of Elliot's Park while playing with his daughters in their favorite park. When Patrick is not inventing more squirrel adventures for Elliot and his friends, you can find him at home in Walla Walla, Washington. He is also the author of the bestselling The Land of Elyon series.

Patrick Carman and Reece Carman in their Halloween costumes.
Photo courtesy of Reece's older sister, Sierra.
Photo © 2008 Sierra Carman